Eeney,
Meeney,
Miney,
Mo

By B.G. Hennessy

Pictures by Letizia Galli

VIKING

The artwork was prepared in ink and watercolor paints.

VIKING
Published by the Penguin Group
Viking Penguin, a division of Penguin Books USA Inc.,
375 Hudson Street, New York, New York 10014, U.S.A.
Penguin Books Ltd, 27 Wrights Lane, London W8 5TZ, England
Penguin Books Australia Ltd, Ringwood, Victoria, Australia
Penguin Books Canada Ltd, 2801 John Street, Markham, Ontario, Canada L3R 1B4
Penguin Books (N.Z.) Ltd, 182–190 Wairau Road, Auckland 10, New Zealand

Penguin Books Ltd, Registered Offices: Harmondsworth, Middlesex, England

First published in 1990 by Viking Penguin, a division of Penguin Books USA Inc.

10   9   8   7   6   5   4   3   2   1

Library of Congress Cataloging in Publication Data
Hennessy, B. G. (Barbara G.)   Eeney, Meeney, Miney, Mo
by B. G. Hennessy; illustrated by Letizia Galli.   p. cm.
   Summary: Eeney, Meeney, Miney, and Mo take a romp
through the jungle, collecting animals as they go along.
   ISBN 0-670-82864-5   [1. Jungle animals—Fiction.]   I. Galli, Letizia, ill. II. Title.
   PZ7.H3914Ee 1990   [E]—dc20   90-31535

Printed in Japan
Set in Novarese Medium

For Kaitlyn, Casey, and Braden
B.G.H.

To Clementina, Ivan, and Cesare
L.G.

Eeney, Meeney, Miney, Mo,
Caught a tiger by the toe.

Eeney, Meeney, Miney, and Mo
Wouldn't let that tiger go
Until he joined them on their chase.
And so began the jungle race.

Up and down and 'round they went,
Till they found an elephant.

They caught a monkey who liked to hum
And chewed banana bubble gum.

They caught a snake with two green eyes
And trapped a croc who told them lies.

They found a parrot whose tail was green
And caught a mouse who liked ice cream.

Fast and fast and faster they chased
Until a lion fierce they faced.

They caught a zebra from Timbuktu
Who politely asked, "How do you do?"

They caught a camel with one big hump
And two kangaroos who couldn't jump.

They found a rhino but let him go
Because he tickled Miney's toe.

They caught a gazelle whose horns were knotted

And a leopard who was polka-dotted.

Now all these animals made quite a crowd,
And the tiger hollered, very loud,
"Eeney! Meeney! Miney! Mo!
It's time for you to let us go!"

Then, one by one, home they went,
Even the big old elephant.